ACTION SPORTS

Kiteboarding

JOANNE MATTERN

SAYVILLE LIBRARY

Rourke
Publishing LLC
Vero Beach, Florida 32964

© 2009 Rourke Publishing LLC

All rights reserved. No part of this book may be reproduced or utilized in any form or by any means, electronic or mechanical including photocopying, recording, or by any information storage and retrieval system without permission in writing from the publisher.

www.rourkepublishing.com

Photo credits: © sashagala: Table of Contents Image; © Mark Stay: Sidebar Art; © Carlos Caetano: page 4; © Sascha Corti: page 5; © Elena Elisseeva: page 6; © Franck Camhi: page 8, 13; © Ulrike Hammerich: page 10; © Kirk Peart Professional Imaging: page 12; © Andre St-Louis: page 14; © Eric Gevaert: page 15, 16; © Alexey Zarubin: page 18, 19; © Alexander Motrenko: page 20

Editor: Kelli L. Hicks

Cover and page design by Nicola Stratford, bdpublishing.com

Library of Congress Cataloging-in-Publication Data

Mattern, Joanne, 1963-
 Kiteboarding / Joanne Mattern.
   p. cm. -- (Action sports)
 ISBN 978-1-60472-396-0
 1. Kite surfing--Juvenile literature. I. Title.
 GV840.K49M38 2009
 797.3--dc22
                                    2008016353

Printed in the USA

CG/CG

TABLE OF CONTENTS

A New and Exciting Sport	4
How Kiteboarding Started	6
Equipment	10
Staying Safe	14
Tricks and Skills	16
Challenging Competitions	20
Meet the Kiteboarders	22
Glossary	23
Index	24

A New and EXCITING Sport

Kiteboarding combines kite flying, surfing, and snowboarding. Kiteboarding is a new sport. It is one of the fastest growing of all the **extreme sports**.

People kiteboard on land, water, or snow. Kiteboarders use large kites to lift themselves high into the air. When they finally come back to Earth, they surf on the ground, the water, or the snow.

The kite pulls the kiteboarder quickly across the snow.

DID YOU KNOW...?

Kiteboarding is sometimes called kitesurfing.

5

How KITEBOARDING Started

In the early 1980s, a man named Cory Roeseler invented a new kind of kite. Roeseler put together a kite and some **water skis**. The kite was very large. It looked like a sail. The rider

When air is pumped into the frame, the frame inflates to hold the kite stiff so it can catch the wind.

held onto wires connected to the kite. As the kite flew, it pulled the rider on water skis. Roeseler called his system the Kiteski. He began to sell it in 1986.

Cory Roeseler was not the only person who knew kites could help people move faster in the water. In 1984, two French brothers named Bruno and Dominique Legaignoux got an exciting idea. They made a new kind of kite. Their kite was made of thin, strong nylon. It had an **inflatable frame**.

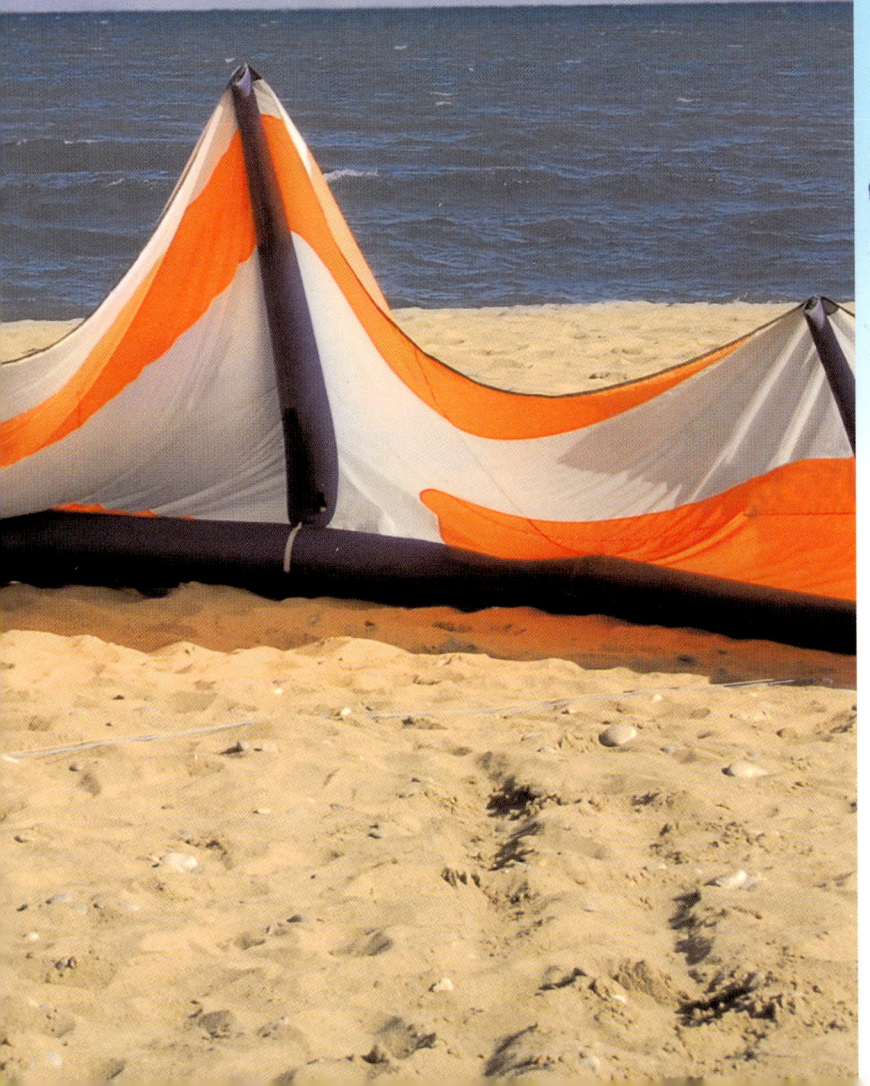

SPEEDY CORY!

Cory Roeseler lives in Oregon. He likes to kiteboard on some of the fast rivers there. Roeseler has set records as the fastest kiteboarder at several races in Oregon.

This kiteboarder uses a hand pump to quickly fill the kite frame.

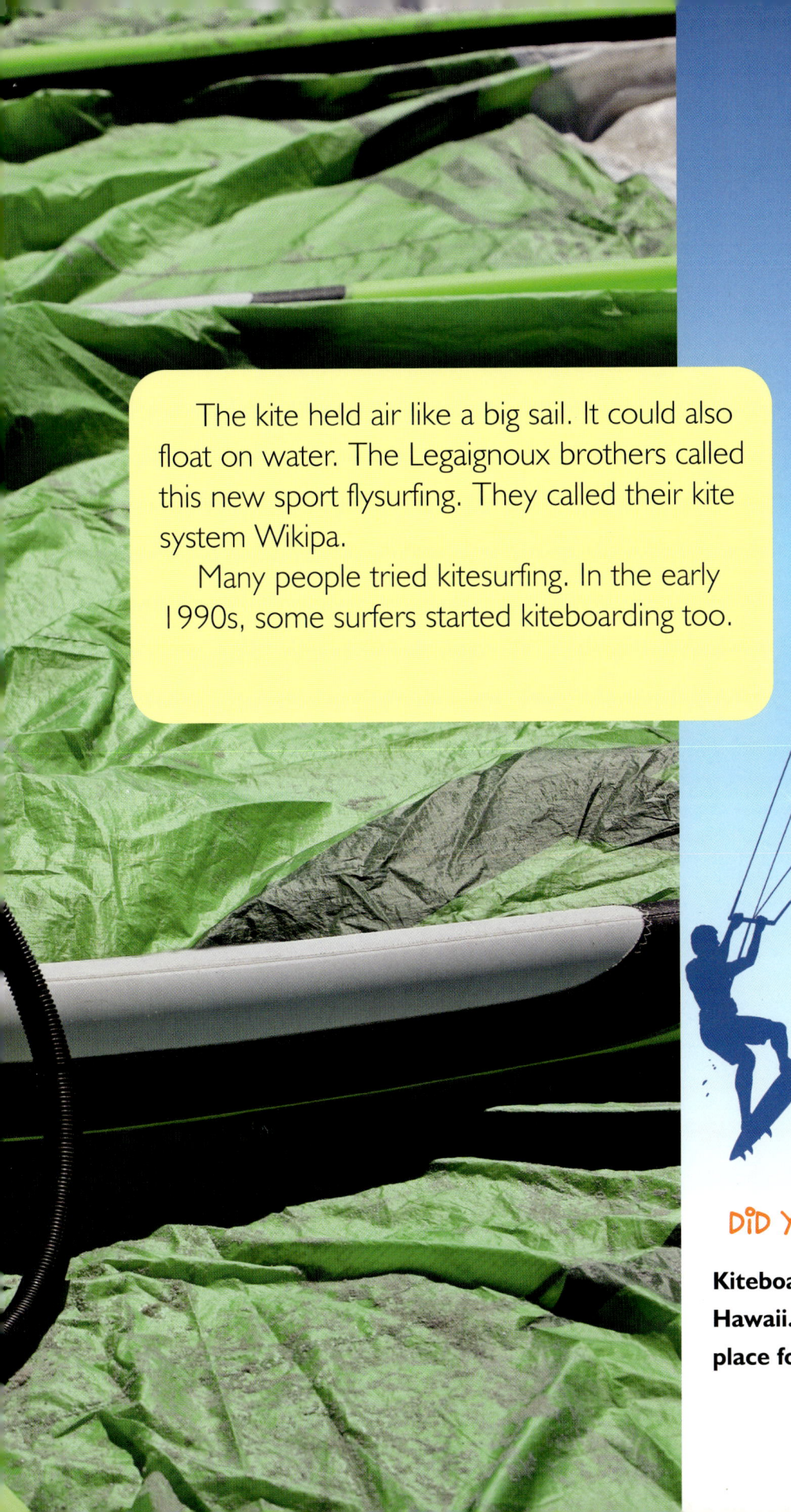

The kite held air like a big sail. It could also float on water. The Legaignoux brothers called this new sport flysurfing. They called their kite system Wikipa.

Many people tried kitesurfing. In the early 1990s, some surfers started kiteboarding too.

DID YOU KNOW...?

Kiteboarding is popular in Hawaii. Hawaii is a popular place for surfing too!

EQUIPMENT

Kiteboarding kites are made of a thin, strong material called nylon.

Kiteboarders need three things to take part in this sport. They need a kite, a board, and a **harness**.

Kiteboarding kites are a lot like **parachutes**. The kites are made of a thin, strong material attached to an inflatable frame. These kites can float on water. They are also very light. The kite and frame only weigh about two pounds (.9 kilogram).

Kiteboarding kites come in different shapes. A low aspect kite is wide. This kind of kite is good for beginners. A high aspect kite is narrow. This kind of kite can travel very fast. It is best for **experienced** kiteboarders.

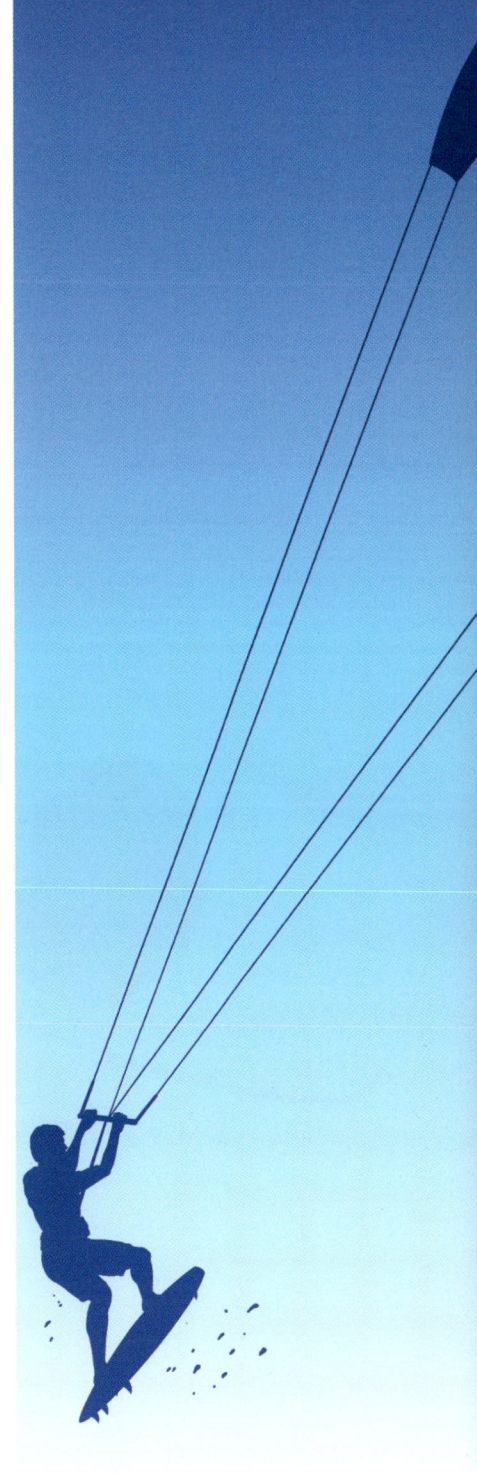

A wakeboard has special straps to hold the rider's feet onto the board.

12

Kiteboards come in different shapes. The most popular is the **wakeboard**. A wakeboard looks like a wide surfboard. It has foot straps to hold the rider onto the board.

Kiteboarders have to hold onto the kite. A kiteboarder wears a harness around his or her waist. This lets the kite pull the rider by the body and not the arms.

Kiteboarders also hold onto a **control bar**. The bar attaches to the kite with wires. Kiteboarders push or pull on the bar to steer the kite.

It takes a lot of arm strength to control a kite using a control bar!

STAYING SAFE

It is safer for kiteboarders to learn this sport on land. A helmet also helps keep the kiteboarder safe.

Kiteboarding can be dangerous. Many kiteboarders go to school to learn how to do this sport. These schools teach kiteboarders how to use their equipment. They teach them how to stay safe.

Kiteboarders must learn to control their kites. They practice for a long time on land. Then they learn how to kiteboard in the water. It takes at least three weeks to learn the **basic** skills of kiteboarding.

Helmets are such an important piece of equipment that some kiteboarders wear them in the water too.

DiD YOU KNOW...?

A safety leash helps a kiteboarder stay safe. The leash is a strap that connects the control bar to the rider's wrist. If the rider lets go of the control bar, the leash pulls on the kite. The kite folds up right away.

SAYVILLE LIBRARY

TRICKS AND SKILLS

The first thing a kiteboarder learns is how to jump. To jump, the rider pulls the control bar into the body. Then he lifts one hand. This lets the kite fill with air. It lifts the rider out of the water.

Kiteboarders also learn to turn their boards. Turning the board into the wind helps the rider jump. Turning the board away from the wind helps the rider land.

WHO GOES FIRST?

If two kiteboarders are close together, who goes first? The kiteboarder whose right hand is forward has the right of way.

A basic kiteboarding trick includes holding the control bar with just one hand.

Sometimes kiteboarders let go of the control bar with one hand. They use this hand to grab the board. Kiteboarders have to hold onto the control bar with the other hand. If they let go, they will lose control. Then the kite will crash.

Experienced kiteboarders can do flips. One of the most exciting flips is the **airpass**. To do an airpass, the kiteboarder flips upside down in the air. Then the kiteboarder twists his body. He turns the board in a spin. Finally, it's time to land in the water.

This kiteboarder flips and twists into an airpass.

CHALLENGING COMPETITIONS

Watch as this kiteboarder sails over the water and does a flip!

If you are a really good kiteboarder, you might take part in a **competition**. Kiteboarders do many exciting tricks during a competition. They do difficult flips and spins. Sometimes they put several flips and spins together to show off. You can see some very exciting tricks in a competition!

Hawaii hosts many kiteboarding competitions. The most exciting is the Red Bull King of the Air contest. The best kiteboarders enter this competition. They do the most **challenging** tricks. The winner of this contest gets a lot of money!

MEET THE KITEBOARDERS

Some kiteboarders have become very popular. Let's meet two of the sport's favorite athletes.

In 1998, **Julie Gilbert** went to Hawaii to **windsurf**. Instead, she learned how to kiteboard. Julie became a great kiteboarder! In 2001, she set the world record for hang time. That's the time a kiteboarder stays in the air. In 2001, Julie was voted the Best Female Kiteboarder. Then, in 2002, Julie broke her own hang time record. Her new record was 6.48 seconds.

Marcus "Flash" Austin won the World Championship of Kiteboarding in 2000. He is famous for all the fancy tricks he does. Marcus holds a very interesting kiteboarding record. He was the first person to kiteboard between Norway and Denmark. That trip was 70 miles (113 kms) long!

GLOSSARY

airpass (AYR-pass): a kiteboarding trick that includes a flip and a spin

basic (BAY-sik): important and fundamental

challenging (CHAL-uhnj-ing): hard to do

competition (kom-puh-TIH-shuhn): a contest

control bar (kuhn-TROHL BAR): a bar that kiteboarders hold to control their kites

experienced (ek-SPEER-ee-uhnssd): skilled

extreme sports (eks-TREME spuhrtz): sports that involve danger and excitement

frame (FRAYM): a structure over which something is built

harness (HAR-nuhss): a device that straps a person to something

inflatable (in-FLAY-tuh-buhl): something that can be filled with air

kiteboarding (KITE-bord-ing): a sport that combines kite flying with surfing, skiing, or skateboarding

parachutes (PA-ruh-shootz): a large piece of fabric attached to thin ropes that lets a person float in the air

wakeboard (WAYK-bord): a wide surfboard

water skis (WAH-tur SKEEZ): skis that are used in the water

windsurf (WIND-surf): to move through water by standing on a board connected to a sail

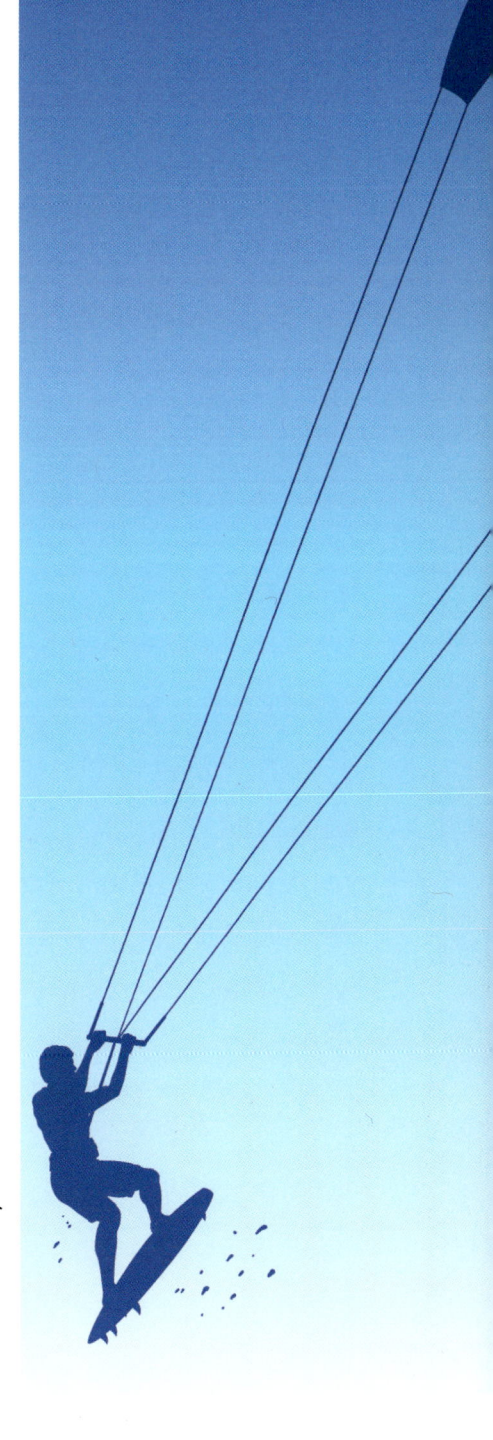

INDEX

Austin, Marcus   21
competition   20, 21
control bar   13, 15, 16, 18
extreme sports   4
flysurfing   9
frame   7, 11
Gilbert, Julie   21
hang time   21
harness   11, 13
Hawaii   9, 21
inflatable   7, 11
kites   4, 6, 7, 11, 13, 15, 16

Kiteski   7
Legaignoux, Bruno   7, 9
Legaignoux, Dominique   7, 9
parachutes   11
Red Bull King of the Air   21
Roeseler, Cory   6, 7
safety leash   15
tricks   16, 17, 18, 19, 20, 21
wakeboard   13
water skis   6, 7
Wikipa   9

FURTHER READING

Preszler. *Kiteboarding*. Capstone Press, 2005.

Voeller, Edward A. *Extreme Surfing*. Capstone Press, 2000.

Woods, Bob. *Water Sports*. Gareth Stevens Publishing, 2004.

WEBSITES

www.kiteboardingmag.com

www.kitesafe.org/kiss_kite2

www.maui.net/~hotwind/kite2.html

ABOUT THE AUTHOR

Joanne Mattern is the author of more than 300 books for children. She has written about a variety of subjects, including sports, history, animals, and science. She loves bringing nonfiction subjects to life for children! Joanne lives in New York State with her husband, four children, and assorted pets.

SAYVILLE LIBRARY
88 GREENE AVENUE
SAYVILLE, NY 11782

APR 2 8 2010

**DISCARDED BY
SAYVILLE LIBRARY**